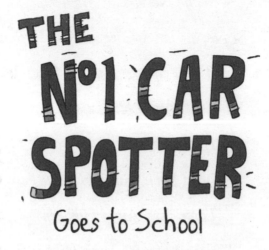

THE No1 CAR SPOTTER

Goes to School

Books by the same author

The No. 1 Car Spotter

The No. 1 Car Spotter and the Firebird

The No. 1 Car Spotter and the Car Thieves

Anna Hibiscus

Hooray for Anna Hibiscus!

Good Luck, Anna Hibiscus!

Have Fun, Anna Hibiscus!

Welcome Home, Anna Hibiscus!

Go Well, Anna Hibiscus!

For younger readers

Anna Hibiscus' Song

Splash! Anna Hibiscus

THE No.1 CAR SPOTTER

Goes to School

by Atinuke

illustrated by Warwick Johnson Cadwell

WALKER
BOOKS

First published in Great Britain 2014 by Walker Books Ltd
87 Vauxhall Walk, London SE11 5HJ

2 4 6 8 10 9 7 5 3 1

Text © 2014 by Atinuke
Illustrations © 2014 Warwick Johnson Cadwell

The right of Atinuke and Warwick Johnson Cadwell to be identified as
author and illustrator respectively of this work has been asserted by them
in accordance with the Copyright, Designs and Patents Act 1988

This book has been typeset in Stempel Schneidler and WJCadwell

Printed and bound in Great Britain by Clays Ltd, St Ives plc

British Library Cataloguing in Publication Data:
a catalogue record for this book is
available from the British Library

ISBN 978-1-4063-4292-5

www.walker.co.uk

For the children of
SOS Children's Villages worldwide
and especially Reindorf and Jennifer
A.

For my gang as usual,
D, S, H and W
W. JC.

No. 1 Catches a Cow

You know me! I'm the No. 1! The No. 1
car spotter in my village. And the No. 1 at
having fun! My village is a poor village lost
in the bush on the continent of Africa. But
there are No. 1 cars that pass on the road.
And I can spot them all!

All day, every day, I am busy spotting cars in the village. While I am herding goats in the bush with my sister, Sissy, and while I am running around collecting firewood for my Grandmother. And especially while I am sitting under the iroko tree with Grandfather.

Spotting cars is what I do best. I can spot a car from the sound of its engine. Even before the road brings it before my eyes, I know what car it is.

It was Grandfather who taught me how to do this. When I was still small I would sit with him watching the No. 1 road carry cars and buses and lorries past our village on their way from one city to another.

"Listen!" Grandfather would say. "You hear that car coming? You hear that noise? *'BRub-BRub-BRub!'*"

I would nod my head until it nearly fell off my neck.

"That be a poor man's car," Grandfather would explain. "Engine farting loud. No shame!"

We would laugh together. Then we would hear another car.

"Aha!" Grandfather would say. "Listen again well-well. You hear that engine?"

Again I would nod.

"'*Purrrrrrrrrr!*'" Grandfather copied the engine sound. "That be a rich man's car, smooth and silent like a leopard fat from eating a poor man's goats!"

Again we would laugh. Then Grandfather would say, "Shhhh! You hear that one? '*Hummmmmmmm!*' That one be king of the road."

And together we would watch an SUV 4Runner pass.

"You see," Grandfather said, staring after the car. "That car tyre pass any hole for road. That cow bar can remove any cow commot for road. And that car body is as big as a house where a man lives with his four wives all together!"

Soon I could recognize any car from the engine sound before I even saw it.

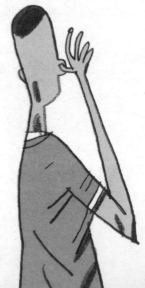

That was how well
I listened.
Hondas.
Peugeots.
BMWs.
V-Boots.
Bedfords. I knew them all!

That was when everybody
started to call me No. 1,
the No. 1 car spotter wey
dey for village.

And now the Chief of Police has declared
me the No. 1 car spotter in the country.
This is because I used my
No. 1 car-spotting
skills to catch a
gang of international
car thieves!

"In fact," I say to my tight friend,
Coca-Cola, "I could be the No. 1 car spotter
in the world!"

Coca-Cola are I are at the river with my sister, Sissy, and her friend Nike. We are watching the cows drink.

My mother's cows are there. Coca-Cola's mother's cows are there. Everybody's cows are there. And we are there too. We are there to make sure that the cows don't cross the shallow river and head for our mothers' fields.

Our white spotted cow is the leader of the whole herd. And that white cow always has one horn pointed in the direction of the fields. She knows well-well that the fields are full of plants sweeter and juicier than the tough dry grass in the bush.

This white cow is so wild and so strong that she has a ring through her nose as if she was an oga-boss and not a madam. We are all afraid of this cow.

Sissy sucks her teeth. "How can you say that?" she asks. "How can you even think that you are the No. 1 car spotter in the whole world?"

I shrug my shoulders.

"I am No. 1 for here, anyway," I say.

"Maybe," says Sissy. "Maybe you are No. 1 in this useless ye-ye village. But you are definitely not No. 1 in London!"

"What do you know about London?" Coca-Cola asks Sissy. Coca-Cola always supports me against sisters and grandmothers. That is what tight friends do. "Have you ever been to London?" he asks.

"I don't need to go to London," Sissy answers. "I don't need to go to London to know that there are cars there that you useless ye-ye boys have never seen before!"

I narrow my eyes at Sissy. Then I hear an engine. "SUV!" I shout. "4Runner! 4Runner!"

Look at that car cruising around the bend! Oh, Grandfather is so, so right. It is indeed king of the road!

"4Runner! 4Runner!" Coca-Cola jumps up and down.

The 4Runner slows. The driver winds down his window and shouts.

Coca-Cola, Sissy, Nike and I look at one another. What is this man saying? He is pulling  the words out of his mouth like Mama making chin-chin cookies.

The driver gets out of his car. He waves his arms and shouts again. Something about a bridge.

I look at Coca-Cola. Should we run to the road and help the man? Maybe he would allow us to look inside his cool-cool car? But what about the cows?

The cows!

Too late I look back to the river. The cows have already crossed it! The white spotted

leader is now marching purposefully in the
direction of the fields. All the other cows
are following her.

I scream the cow call. It calls the cows to
water. But the cows do not listen. They are no
longer thirsty. They have drunk all they want
and are headed for the sweet, juicy fields.

If the cows eat our crops, what will we
eat this year? We will starve. But before we
starve, our mothers will kill us!

I start to run after the cows.
Behind me, Coca-Cola
is running too.
Suddenly my
foot hits a stone
in the river. I fall.
My hands and
knees hit rocks.
Water enters
my mouth.

By the time I sit up in the river, Coca-Cola
is jumping up
and down in
front of the white
cow. He is shouting
and waving a stick.
Na-wa-oh! I think, as
river water drips down my
face. Coca-Cola must be more
afraid of his mother than he
is of that white cow.

I do not have any more time to think.
The white cow turns. She leads the cows
stampeding towards me, their horns and
hooves flying. There is no time to move out
of their way. They are going to trample me!

I close my eyes. The ground shakes as the
cows pass by. Water splashes me. And I am
still alive!

Then I hear Sissy and Nike scream! I open my eyes and look around. Sissy and Nike are running away from the charging cows. They are too afraid of their tossing horns and wild rolling eyes to stand their ground and stop them.

The SUV driver is standing by his car with his mouth wide open. Sissy and Nike are running towards him. Soon the cows with their sharp horns and their stampeding hooves will be upon him too!

I jump up and run after the cows. I can see nothing over their backs. But I can hear Sissy and Nike screaming. And I can hear the 4Runner driver shouting too.

My legs put on speed. I overtake the stubborn black cow and the cow with curled horns. My legs go for world record speed. That cow is fast, but I know my legs are faster. As fast as an Olympic Gold winner!

Suddenly I
am level with
the white
cow. I dive
underneath her
horns and catch
her nose ring.
She bellows
and brakes.
She skids along
the road on
splayed hooves
and together we
crash into the SUV.

The other cows are running in circles
around us now, tossing their horns and
bellowing. But the white spotted
cow is silent. While I hold
her ring I am her master, even
lying on the ground under the
4Runner.

But where is Sissy? And where is Nike? Why can I not hear them? Are they behind me, lying trampled in the road?

Slowly I get up. Sissy and Nike have their faces pressed against the windows of the SUV. They are inside!

I am so surprised I jump and nearly let go of the white cow! Sissy and Nike start to laugh. Coca-Cola runs up. We are all laughing now. The cows did not eat our mothers' crops. And nobody got trampled.

The head of the SUV driver appears over the edge of the SUV roof. He is staring at the cows and at us.

Quickly we stop laughing. Will this man be angry with us for not controlling our cows? And with Sissy and Nike for entering his car?

He jumps down from the roof. His white shirt and blue jeans are covered with red dust. His mouth is still open. Suddenly he takes my hand. He shakes it. And then again, and again, like a woman at a water pump.

"I cannot thank you enough! I cannot thank you enough!"

Is that really what he is saying?

Suddenly the man drops my hand. His hand goes to his other arm. He removes his watch. A big, heavy, shiny American watch. He straps it onto my arm. I cannot believe my eyes.

"Thank you, sa," I whisper.

"You deserve it, son!" The man puts his hand onto my head. "You are a brave young man. Very brave."

Sissy and Nike jump down from the SUV and stare at the watch. I feel so proud. I can see Coca-Cola eying it.

"American..." Coca-Cola touches the watch.

The man smiles proudly and touches his chest.

"American!" he says.

An American as black as an African! Wait until I tell Grandfather this! So that is why he pulls words out of his mouth like Mama making chin-chin!

"Is that your village?"

The American points down the road. You can just see the village, and the iroko tree, and the cows corral.

We all nod.

"Jump in," says the American. "I will give y'all a ride back."

Coca-Cola and Sissy and Nike and I look at one another. Can this be for true? Are we being invited to ride in the coolest car on the road?

I gesture
to the white
cow. I dare
not let go of her
nose ring. The
American takes a
rope from the back of
his vehicle. I use it to tie
the cow to the back of the
SUV. Then I jump straight in!

Everybody in the village runs down to
the road when they see the cows being
led slowly along by an SUV 4Runner. And
when they see all of us inside, their eyes
nearly pop out of their heads!

I lift the arm with the American watch
in salute.

"*Na-wa-oh*, No. 1!" shouts my cousin
Emergency.

"*Na-wa-oh*, No. 1!" shouts my cousin
Tuesday.

"*Na-wa-oh*, No. 1!" shouts Uncle Go-Easy.

I jump out of the SUV. Sissy unties the
white cow. The American drives away,
waving and blaring his horn.

I am the No. 1 car spotter. I am also good at catching cows. I have a best friend called Coca-Cola. And a No. 1 American watch!

No. 1 Plays a Game

I am the No. 1 car spotter. I have a best friend called Coca-Cola, a new friend who is an American and a No. 1 American watch!

But none of these things can save me from Grandmother!

"Lazy boy! Where are you? Do you hear me?"

Grandmother shouts loud enough for the whole village to hear her.

"Did I not ask you to collect firewood for me?"

Before Grandmother catches sight of me, I jump over the back wall of the compound. I run down to Mama Coca-Cola's chop-house restaurant. My best friend, Coca-Cola, is here, pushing a wheelbarrow of soft drinks. He is helping his mother with her akara bean fritter business. Hungry akara eaters drink a lot of Coca-Cola!

Coca-Cola smiles as I skid around the corner.

"Grandmother wahalla?" he asks.

"Big wahalla," I pant.

Then I hear an engine...

"4Runner!" I shout. "4Runner! 4Runner!"

The big shiny SUV parks in front of the chophouse. It is the SUV belonging to the American who gave me this same watch.

The American climbs down from his mighty car with a mighty smile.

"Welcome, *oga*, welcome!" I shout.

"Hello, No. 1." The American shakes my hand as if I were a big man.

He opens the back door of his vehicle. Inside there is a boy looking at a computer game.

"Come on, son," the American says.

"Hang on!"

The boy does not even look at his father.

"Come on, son," the American says again. "I want you to meet somebody."

"I'm busy!" The boy's eyes are fixed on the game.

Coca-Cola and I look at each other. I have never heard a son answer his father like this!

"Son!" The American begins to put some stick in his voice. "I want you to meet the boy who saved my life."

"OK, Dad, OK." The boy sighs. "Keep cool."

The boy climbs down from the car.

"This is No. 1." The American introduces me. "And his friend Coca-Cola."

The boy glances up at us only quickly. His eyes are still locked on his game. The American sighs.

"This is my son—" he begins.

"Dad, I'm thirsty," the boy interrupts.

The American rubs his hands together.

"Let's all have a drink," he says.

Coca-Cola and I are quick to follow the American and his son into the chop-house. We sit down as if we are used to being served soft drinks every day. Mama Coca-Cola puts her hands on her hips and purses her lips. The American waves a note big enough to buy the whole village soft drinks. Mama Coca-Cola smiles.

"Dad, I'm hungry." The boy complains without even looking at his father.

"Akara?" asks Mama Coca-Cola.

The American leans towards his son and says a few words in his ear. The only word I catch is "germs".

"Sorry," Mama Coca-Cola says sorrowfully. "We don't sell germs here. Only akara."

"But it is the finest akara in the whole country!" Coca-Cola says truthfully.

The American looks embarrassed. He shakes his head. "Maybe not today," he says.

His son groans and rolls his eyes. Coca-Cola and I look at each other again. Have you ever seen a boy so rude to his own father?

Coca-Cola and I swallow our cold drinks. Then we belch loudly. We want the American to know how much we appreciate the drinks he has bought us!

For one second the American boy looks
up at us from his game. He snorts and curls
his lip. Who can understand such a boy?

I follow his eyes down to the computer
game. His thumbs are pumping fast on tiny
buttons. I sometimes see these machines
in the back of air-conditioned cars as I run
along beside them. They are always in the
hands of boys and girls who do not even
look at me.

But I have never seen such a game so close before. I lean closer and closer and see a BMW motor-car driving fast along a road. Suddenly it collides with the road barriers. It turns and catches on fire!

"Argh!" I shout and clutch my head.

But then the same car reappears, unbroken! My eyes open wide. What kind of magic ju-ju is this?

The boy is still staring at the screen. His thumbs work fast on the buttons.

The BMW speeds down the road again. The boy's thumbs are controlling the car!

"Go! Go! Go!" I shout.

The car speeds faster and faster. As fast as the boy's thumbs. Suddenly it crashes and burns.

"No!" I raise my hands to my head again.

The boy looks up at me. He smiles.

His father speaks. "Son, I have to go and inspect the bridge."

"Boring!" says the boy.

"Why don't you stay here?" The American smiles. "With your new friends."

"Sure." The boy shrugs.

"I will get your bag for you." The American pats his son's shoulder.

I catch Coca-Cola's eye.

A father fetching and carrying his son's bag? Is everything upside down in America? Is it because the world is round and America is on the other side?

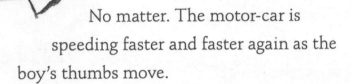

No matter. The motor-car is

speeding faster and faster again as the

boy's thumbs move.

"Go! Go! GO!" Coca-Cola and I are both shouting.

Suddenly a red light flashes on the screen.

"Shoot!" says the boy.

He puts the game down on the table. He pulls an electric plug and lead out of a bag.

The bag! I had not noticed his father drop it off. I had not thanked him for the cold drink, or said goodbye to him, or wished him well with his work.

How easy it is to become rude like this

American boy, I think! It takes only one small computer game.

The boy is looking around the chop-house. "Where can I plug in the charger?" he asks.

Coca-Cola and I look at each other.

The boy waves the plug. "Plug! Plug!" he says.

I look at Coca-Cola again. "No electricity," I say at last.

The boy looks at me and frowns. "Say what?" he says.

"No electricity," I say louder.

"What?" the boy shouts. "None at all?"

"At-all, at-all." Coca-Cola shrugs his shoulders.

The boy groans. He beats his fist on the table. Mama Coca-Cola eyes us.

"Coca-Cola! No. 1! Take the cows to the river!" she shouts. "Now-now!"

"Yes, Ma," says Coca-Cola quickly. We turn to run out of the door.

"And take that boy with you!" Mama Coca-Cola shouts.

"Yes, Ma," Coca-Cola answers again.

"Come!" I call the boy.

"Electricity?" he asks hopefully.

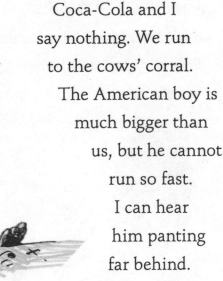

Coca-Cola and I say nothing. We run to the cows' corral. The American boy is much bigger than us, but he cannot run so fast. I can hear him panting far behind.

When he reaches the corral, we have
already opened the gate.

The cows are pouring out, shaking their
horns and stamping their legs. The flies are
biting them. The cows are thirsty and bad-
tempered.

"Whoa!" says the boy, panting.

Then he asks, "Was that your mother
shouting at you? I would not let my mother
shout at me like that."

Coca-Cola and I say nothing. This boy comes from an upside down world, where sons argue with their fathers and fathers carry bags for their sons. And mothers don't shout. Maybe it is the sons that shout at their mothers? What do I know?

I throw a small stone to the left of the cows. It makes them turn right, towards the river. Coca-Cola and I follow slowly. Soon the cows have their mouths in the water. Only their tails move now.

"God, it's boring here." The American boy kicks the stones. "Is this all you have to do? No electricity, no mall. What a dump!"

Coca-Cola's eyes flick to me. We don't answer. We keep our eyes on the cows.

The white spotted cow raises her head and tosses her horns. She is the leader, and she has finished drinking. It is time to go back to the corral. Before she thinks up trouble.

I throw a stone in front of the cow. Coca-Cola throws one to her right. The white cow turns left, back towards the corral. The others follow. The corral gate is open. All the cows have to do is enter.

"This is for babies!" says the American boy suddenly. "A baby could look after these cows. What we need here is some action!"

He bends down and picks up a handful of stones. He throws them at the cows and shouts, "Yee-ha!"

The stones land on both sides of the cows. They panic. Instead of going in through the gate, they begin to run around the corral.

The American boy laughs. He chases after them, throwing more stones.

Faster and faster the cows run around the corral. Suddenly the American boy is not behind the cows. The cows are behind him! Now the boy is no longer laughing. He is running for his life!

Coca-Cola looks at me. I look at Coca-Cola. One or two stones from us could make the cows enter the corral.

"He wanted action..." I say slowly.

Coca-Cola nods.

The white cow catches up with the boy. She flings him into the air. The boy flies over her head and lands on her back like an American cowboy.

Coca-Cola and I cheer.

"That's what I call action!" I laugh.

Then somebody grabs one of my ears. It is Grandmother. She tries to raise me off the ground by my ear.

"Do you want to kill that boy?" she shouts. "Has all sense left your body?"

I am too busy following my ear to answer. But Coca-Cola throws a stone. The cows enter the corral. Coca-Cola runs to shut the gate. The American boy is lying on the ground, groaning. And Grandmother is still shaking my ear!

"Stupid!"

Her voice broadcasts for the whole village to hear.

"Foolish!"

Grandmother draws breath.

"Ignorant!"

"Excuse me, ma'am," says a small voice behind her.

Grandmother turns swiftly, dragging me with her.

It is the American boy. My eyes widen. This boy has got up and dared to interrupt Grandmother. And Grandmother is far more dangerous than cows! Especially when interrupted in her most important job of controlling grandsons.

"Please, ma'am," says the American boy. "It was me. I convinced your boys that I could control the cows. It was all my fault."

Coca-Cola's mouth drops open.
Grandmother's fingers let go of my ear.
She reaches out her hand.

I close my eyes. If Grandmother slaps
this American boy it could cause an
international incident!

Grandmother chuckles. I open my eyes.
Grandmother is
pinching the American
boy's cheek. Hard.
This is an
accepted way
to greet a child.
It hurts. But it
is considered
friendly.

Grandmother chuckles again. "It takes
an African boy to control those cows," she
says.

"Yes, ma'am." The American boy squirms.
"I sure know that now, ma'am."

Grandmother lets go of the American boy's cheek. Coca-Cola and I grab his arms. We race away before Grandmother can do or say anything else. When we reach the safety of the chop-house, we stop running. We let go of his arms.

The boy looks at us and we look at him. Suddenly he grins. He put out his hand. "LeRoy," he says.

"No. 1," I say.

"Cool name," LeRoy says. "Good to meet you, bro."

LeRoy surprises me with a fancy handshake. He does the same to Coca-Cola. Then he shakes his head.

"Wow!" he says. "If my mother shouted like that, I would jump to obey her before she even opened her mouth."

Mama Coca-Cola hears what he says and looks at him approvingly.

"Food now?" she asks.

"Yes, ma'am!" LeRoy answers.

Mama Coca-Cola puts a mountain of akara in front of the three of us. LeRoy finishes more than Coca-Cola and me put together. Just then his father walks through the door. He sees the plate with akara crumbs in front of us. LeRoy opens his mouth. A loud belch comes out. The American's eyes open wide.

"LeRoy!" He sounds shocked.

Mama Coca-Cola smiles. Coca-Cola and I smile too.

For a while, the computer game turned us all into American boys. But we have our own magic ju-ju here in the village too.

One small plate of our akara bean fritters can turn an American boy into an African boy in less than than the time it takes to eat them!

Na-wa-oh!

No. 1 Chases a Story

"No. 1!" It is my sister, Sissy, shouting.

"No. 1!" Coca-Cola is shouting too.

"No. 1!" Even Mama Coca-Cola is
shouting.

I jump down from the palm tree
and run to the chop-house. What
happen now?

Outside the chop-house the Firebird is parked. It is the car of one famous professor. He happens to be a friend of mine.

"Welcome, Prof," I greet him inside the chop-house.

"Good news, No. 1!" Prof smiles. He shakes his newspaper and reads aloud. "Thanks to a young girl..."

My eyes widen. I recognize that girl in the picture! She lives in the city, but her family originally come from a village near here.

Prof reads the whole story. That girl had been teaching the children in her village to read and to write. Those children proved to be very clever. But the girl could not keep teaching them because she had to go back to her home in the city. Now the government has promised to build a school for those cleva-cleva children.

"'... and for all children in the surrounding area.'"

Prof stops reading. Coca-Cola and Sissy
are staring at me with shining eyes. Why?
Then I realize!

This is the surrounding area of that girl's
village! This is where the government is
building a school! A school for us!

Suddenly I am shouting and dancing around the chop-house with Sissy and Coca-Cola. Mama Coca-Cola leaves her cooking fires and comes to dance. She calls Mama, and soon she is dancing too. Even Grandmother dances when she hears the news.

I can hoe fields and carry the harvest to market. I can collect palm nuts for oil and throw nets for fish. I can herd goats and cows. I can find solutions to leopards and floods and car thefts. I can tell a Benz from a BMW before I even see it. I can tell the year of a Bedford just from the rattle of its engine. And I know if the car approaching is a taxi or a personal Peugeot from the dust that it kicks up. I am the No. 1 car spotter. And here in my village I know everything that I need to know.

But there are two things which I cannot do at-all, at-all. I cannot read. And I cannot write.

And everybody knows that to have an important job and drive fine-fine cars, a person has to be able to read and write.

And I want to be a big man. I want to have an important job, and I want to drive fine-fine cars. But more than this, I want to be able to read books.

The American boy, LeRoy, comes here every week now. He brings his Nintendo DS and we play computer games until the power expires. After that we eat a mountain of akara. And after that LeRoy takes from his bag one book after another. And he reads aloud so that we can enjoy together, he and Coca-Cola and I.

Inside his books are stories of boys who work as spies for the British secret service, boys who are foolish enough to steal wicked rings, boys who fight great magicians who cannot be named and boys who have to decide between following a witch or a lion.

And, na-wa-oh, those stories-o! Once LeRoy starts to read them I no longer know that I am sitting in the chop-house.

I no longer know whether it is time to take the cows to the river or time to collect firewood for the cooking fires. I cannot even hear Grandmother shout when she is standing in the door of the chop-house!

Once those stories enter my brain I know nothing else. I cannot sleep at night, I cannot eat my food. One time I even got lost in the bush because I was thinking of them.

Will the boy who is a spy die? Will the Hobbit boy who carries the ring escape from its curses? And will the lion who defeated the witch eat the boy who betrayed him?

I, too, was once a spy, lying on the floor of a car thieves' car. I know what it is to fear death.

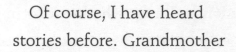

Of course, I have heard
stories before. Grandmother
tells Sissy and me
stories when the
moon is bright
and nobody
can sleep.
She tells us
funny stories of animals who can speak;
and who do the ill-advised things that Sissy
and I always want to do.

Grandfather tells stories
too. In fact, many
people come to hear
Grandfather recite
stories under the
iroko tree. They
bring cloth and goats
and stew and money
to pay Grandfather
for his stories.

But it is the stories inside
LeRoy's books that I would
pay for! I love those stories.
Inside each one is a boy
like me!

"Take the books,"
LeRoy is always saying to me.
"Read them for yourself."

I shake my head and say nothing. I do
not want LeRoy to know that I cannot
read. A big boy like me should be able to
read. For a long time I have been able to
stretch my hand over my head and touch
my opposite ear. This means that I am old
enough to go to school. Except that there is
no school to go to.

But there will be one soon!

"School! School! School!" Sissy and Coca-Cola and I are shouting and screaming.

Prof is smiling at us.

Our mothers and grandmothers are singing.

"Our children will go to school!
Our children will go to school!
Now-now they will talk
for us in the court.
Now-now they will talk
for us in the hospital.
Now-now they will talk
for us in the government.
Our children will go to school!"

Grandfather hobbles down
from the iroko tree to see
what the noise is all about.
I see him standing in the
doorway of the chop-house
leaning on his stick. I see
Mama run to talk to him.
I see sorrow strike his face.
Grandfather turns to go.
I stop dancing. What is the
matter with
Grandfather?
Then Sissy
catches hold
of my hands.

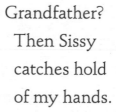

"We will go to school,
No. 1!" she shouts.
"We will go together!"
And I immediately
join her in dancing and
shouting again.

The next day, Uncle Go-Easy goes to
where the school is being built. He finds
out everything.

"It is true!" he says when he returns to
the village. "They have almost completed
the school!

"It will be free, and any child in the area
can attend," he explains. "But the children
must provide their own school uniform and
their own pencils and their own exercise
books."

Sissy and I look at each other. Coca-Cola's mother will have plenty of money for uniforms and pencils because she is a chop-madam. But what about us?

Mama smiles when she sees our faces.

"No. 1," she says. "Have you forgotten your reward?"

When I helped the Chief of Police to catch the car thieves, he gave me a big reward, which I gave to Mama to look after.

"There is plenty of money for uniforms and pencils and books, and even shoes, for both of you!" Mama says.

Sissy and I scream with joy. I run to the iroko tree to tell Grandfather all about it. Maybe he was worried yesterday that we were happy for nothing. Maybe he knew there would be things we would have to pay for. Maybe he thought that we would not have enough money.

 Under the iroko tree
Grandfather is busy.
He is reciting a long
story to a woman. It is
a story that I have not
heard before. I sit near the tree to listen.
I love Grandfather's stories. They are about
our wise ancestors and about our foolish
ancestors and about the gods who were the
ancestors of our ancestors.

The woman nods and nods as
Grandfather is reciting. She wipes away
the tears that run down her face. When he
has finished, she gives him a small bundle
of beautiful cloth. Grandfather thanks her.
Then she goes away.

"How many stories do you know,
Grandfather?" I ask.

Grandfather smiles. "Well," he says. "The
stories I know are divided into groups."

I wait for him to explain.

"Take four and double it," he says.

I nod. A goat has four legs. So he is talking about the number of legs of two goats.

"Now double it again."

Again I nod: the legs of four goats now.

"And again," says Grandfather.

The legs of eight goats. Then the legs of sixteen goats. Then the legs of thirty-two goats. Then the legs of sixty-four goats.

"That many," says Grandfather. "That is how many groups of stories in the Odu Ifa. That is how many stories I know."

I look at Grandfather with wide eyes. He knows more stories than that many legs! How many more stories?

"But as for how many stories there are in each group..." Grandfather shrugs. "I do not know how many. It would take too long to count. And I have never bothered."

I look at Grandfather with my mouth hanging open.

He laughs. "Did you not know that a brain could contain so much?"

I touch my head. It is so small. How could it hold all that?

Grandfather smiles. "It is a mystery," he says. Then he begins to recite again. "The eagle was the first messenger. He was entrusted with an egg..."

Ah! This is one of the best stories!
I have heard Grandfather tell it many times
before. I join him in reciting it. When
I misremember, he stops to correct me.
Then we continue together.

We recite story after story. I did not know
that I knew so many! I sit so often with
Grandfather under the iroko tree while he
is reciting them that they have actually
entered my head!

When we have finished reciting, we are
both very happy. Much time has passed.

The road is quiet. Smoke is
rising from the cooking fires
in the compounds. Soon it
will be time to eat.

Grandfather looks at
me. "You came to tell me
something," he says.

I had forgotten.

Now I remember.

"Grandfather, I am going to school," I say.

Sorrow strikes Grandfather's face again.

"Grandfather!" I take his hand. "What is the matter?"

Grandfather sighs deeply. He passes his other hand across his face.

"School will swallow you up and spit you out in the city," Grandfather says. "The city that has taken all of my sons!"

I am silent. It is true. My father is there. And my uncles. And if I want to look for an important job and fine-fine cars, then I must go there too.

"I will take you, Grandfather," I say. "I will not leave you behind."

Grandfather smiles at me sadly.

"But what if I do not wish to come, No. 1?" Grandfather asks.

I look at Grandfather. He looks at me. The road is quiet. Smoke is rising from the cooking fires in the compounds.

But we are no longer happy. There is sorrow in Grandfather's heart.

I am the No. 1 car spotter. I have an invention and a solution for many things. But sorrow is the hardest thing to beat.

I have done it before, like when Mama Coca-Cola did not like her new house. And when Grandfather was afraid that Grandmother would die. And when a leopard was eating Grandmother's goats.

All of those times I found a way to beat sorrow. I will beat it again this time. I will beat it for Grandfather. Somehow.

No. 1 Goes to School

Today I am so happy. I am so happy because today I go to school.

Last week my mother and I went to town to buy my school uniform. I was so proud. I knew that soon I would be a boy in a uniform carrying books. Everybody would know as I walked along frowning that I was contemplating serious questions. That I was on my way to becoming an important man. Now today is the day I go to school.

"Hurry!" my sister, Sissy, hisses.

The cock has not yet crowed, but Sissy is already impatient.

"We will be late!" she worries.

The school is far. We have to start walking early. Outside in the compound Mama has already lit a fire. She wants us to eat before our long walk. The air is still cool. As we are eating, the cock crows.

"Le's go!" says Sissy.

Mama smiles at Sissy and me. We are both wearing our new uniforms and carrying our new books.

"I am so proud of you both," Mama says.

Grandmother sucks her teeth.

"Wait to hear what the teacher thinks," she says. "Then you will know whether to be proud of them or not!"

Sissy and I run down to the road. Coca-Cola is waiting for us there. Nike too. More and more children join us along the road.

Some of us have shoes and some do not. But we all look fine in our new uniforms. And we all feel proud and happy. We are ready for important things with our uniforms and pencils and empty exercise books.

Soon the sun rises. The air becomes hot. The red dust from the road rises too. Sweat runs down our faces. Dust sticks to the sweat. Sweat runs down our backs. Our uniforms stick to our skin. Dust sticks to our uniforms. Inside my new shoes my feet are paining me. The road to school is long!

By the time we get there none of us look so fine or feel so happy. A tall, skinny woman is waiting outside. When she sees us she sighs. She makes us line up in front of the school. It is a new building made from concrete blocks and corrugated iron. Just like Mama Coca-Cola's chop-house.

The woman tells us that she is our teacher. Her name is Mrs Correction.

Inside, many small tables and benches are crammed together. Mrs Correction makes the girls sit on one side of the room and the boys on the other. Sissy and Nike crowd around a table with some other girls. Coca-Cola and I squeeze onto a bench with some boys from another village.

Mrs Correction has a stick. She uses it to bang on her table until we are all quiet.

"Repeat after me!" Mrs Correction shouts. "ONE!"

"ONE!" we all shout back.

"TWO!"

"TWO!" we all shout back.

"THREE!"

"THREE!" we all shout back.

"FOUR!"

"FOUR!"

"FIVE!"

"FIVE!"

And we continue until …

"TEN!" shouts Mrs Correction.

"TEN!" we all shout back.

"AGAIN!" shouts Mrs Correction.

It is hot in the classroom. I am sweating.
If I was in the village I would be high in
a palm tree, feeling its sweet breeze and
counting cars on the road.

"AGAIN!" shouts Mrs Correction.

Grandfather taught me how to count a
long time ago. How could a village boy herd
goats or spot cars without knowing many,
many numbers?

Grandfather will be sitting under the
iroko tree spotting cars now. He will be
reciting more stories than sixty-four goats
have legs. Which is more than two hundred
and fifty-six.

"OK!" shouts the teacher. "Who can add one plus one?"

It is so hot and so boring that I put my head down on the table.

Suddenly there is a loud crack by my ear. Mrs Correction is standing at my table, shouting that I am rude and lazy to put my head down when she is trying to get something into my thick skull.

By the time school finishes, I am even hotter. And not only are my feet paining me. My backside is paining me too, from sitting on that hard hard chair all day.

We all walk home very slowly. Not only do we not look fine, we do not feel fine either.

When we return to the village, Mama and Grandmother and Mama Coca-Cola are waiting for us. They are eager to hear about our important day. I let Sissy speak about school. I say nothing.

Then we have to wash our dusty
uniforms and hang them out to dry
for tomorrow. We have to take
the cows to water.
We have to
run to collect
firewood and
sweep the compound.
We have to do all the
jobs that Mama and
Grandmother did
not have time
to do while we
were at school.

I do not see Grandfather until
he enters the compound at night to eat.
His footsteps are slow and heavy. His head
is bowed. He does not look at me.

The next day the teacher teaches us
something new.

a b c d e f g h i j k l m n o p q r s t u v w x y z

Is this the magic ju-ju that will enable me
to read LeRoy's books?

I repeat it again and again with all the
other children. Soon I can even repeat it
backwards when the others are repeating
it forwards.

z y x w v u t s r q p o n m l k j i h g f e d c b a

Then we go back to 1-2-3.

I put my head down on the table.

Mrs Correction's stick
lands beside my head.
She is shouting again!

I have given up Grandfather and the village, and for what? In order to be punished for already knowing what the teacher has to teach.

I miss Grandfather. I miss his stories. He always has something new to teach me. He never punishes me or calls me lazy.

Now there is sorrow in *my* heart too.

It pains me worse than my shoe-broken feet. Worse than my bench-broken backside. Worse than my repetition-broken head.

The next day Mrs Correction asks, "Who can repeat 1 to 10?"

All the children raise their hands.

But when she asks, "Who can repeat A to Z?", it is only me who raises my hand.

Mrs Correction looks at me with raised eyebrows.

I repeat *a b c d e f g h i j k l m n o p q r s t u v w x y z*.

By the time I have finished, Mrs Correction's eyebrows are touching her hair weave. Maybe she'd thought that only stupid boys put their heads down on their tables.

"We will all repeat together until each of you can repeat as well as No. 1," Mrs Correction says.

This time when I put my head down on the table Mrs Correction lets me.

The following day is Saturday. No school. Grandfather calls me to sit under the iroko tree. We spot cars together in the breeze. Nobody forces me to do anything.

I spot the SUV of LeRoy's father. It stops by the chop-house. When LeRoy sees where I am sitting, he runs up to the iroko tree.

"How was school?" LeRoy pants.

I shake my head. I do not want to talk about school.

"What did you learn?" LeRoy asks.

Both Grandfather and LeRoy are looking at me. Slowly I recite the alphabet.

LeRoy looks at me with wide eyes.

"No. 1," he says, "you didn't know that already?"

I shake my head bitterly and look down at≈the ground. There is silence. I can hear the goats bleating far away in the bush.

"I did not know you could not read," says LeRoy slowly.

Then he says, "Now that you know the alphabet, you will soon read. Then you can borrow all of my books!"

I look at LeRoy.

"Let me show you," he says.

LeRoy scratches a mark in the dust. He tells me that this is the letter A that I have learned to recite. He shows me the letter in one of his books. It appears many-many times on each page.

I spend the rest of the day scratching marks in the dust. Soon I can even scratch small words, like "me".

Grandfather watches us intently.

"Can these marks write any word?" he asks.

"Yes," says LeRoy.

"Words in my own language?" Grandfather asks.

"Yes," says LeRoy.

A little light appears in Grandfather's eyes.

"Any word at all?" Grandfather asks.

"Any word," says LeRoy.

The next day is Sunday. Still no school. Again I sit with Grandfather under the iroko tree. I sigh as we spot cars. Tomorrow is school.

"What is it, No. 1?" Grandfather asks at last. "You don't want to learn to read anymore?"

"I want to learn to read," I say. "I just do not like school. I prefer the village."

Grandfather sighs. He looks at the horizon.

"You must go," Grandfather says at last. "You must go to school so that before I die you can write every story from the Odu Ifa that I know. So they will not die with me."

I look at Grandfather. He has never mentioned dying before!

Grandfather pats my hand.

"I will not die soon," he says. "You have time to learn everything."

"But I do not want to go to school!" I start

to cry. "It is so boring. The teacher makes us repeat and repeat even after I have finished learning everything. If I stay there my head will become so heavy it will fall off my shoulders!"

Grandfather pats my hand again.

"I want to stay in the village with you, Grandfather," I cry. "I want to sit here under the iroko tree and recite the Odu Ifa stories, just like you!"

Grandfather stops patting my hand.

"What did you say, No. 1?" he asks.

"I want to learn the Odu Ifa," I say.

I stop crying. Suddenly I know that this is what I want to do. More than I want to be a big man, I want to know the Odu Ifa.

Grandfather looks at me with shining eyes.

"For true, No. 1?" he asks.

I nod my head hard.

"I have been waiting to hear you say that for a long time, No. 1," Grandfather says softly.

"You are the only one of all my sons and grandsons with a brain big enough for the job! And now that you know it is what you want too, I can teach you everything I know."

"And I will not have to go to school any more?" I ask.

Grandfather laughs.

"Of course you must go," he says. "How will you record everything you learn from me if you do not go?"

I look at Grandfather. Now he wants me to go to school?

"Don't worry, No. 1." Grandfather smiles. "You will need all the time you can get to recite all that I will teach you. You can do that at school with your head on your table. How would you do it here, with Grandmother shouting your name from morning to night?"

Grandfather starts to laugh. I am laughing too. We cannot stop.

I am the No. 1 car spotter. I have solutions for leopards, for floods, for houses. And like I told you, I have solutions for sorrow too!

Atinuke was born in Nigeria
and grew up in both Africa and the UK.
She works as a traditional oral storyteller
in schools and theatres all over the world.
All of Atinuke's many children's books
are set in modern Africa. She lives
on a mountain overlooking the sea
in West Wales.

Warwick Johnson Cadwell
lives by the Sussex seaside with his
smashing family and pets. Most of
his time is spent drawing, or thinking
about drawing, but for a change of
scenery he also skippers boats.
The No. 1 Car Spotter Goes to School
is his sixth book for Walker Books.